Characters

Yellow-headed Blackbird

Red-headed Woodpecker

Mallard

Hooded Merganser

Scarlet Tanager

Marbled Godwit

Ruddy Duck

Rubber Duckie

Robin

Painted Bunting

American White Pelican

Sept. 2020

Uh-Oh! We've Got Birds!

By
Peter Ross

To Harrison & Eloise
May you soar with
Oliver & Mabel &
their friends!
Pete Ross

Beaver's Pond Press
Saint Paul, Minnesota

About Peter Ross

Uh-Oh! We've Got Birds! is the first book by Peter Ross, and it's no surprise that it involves birds. Pete has loved nature, especially birds, for as long as he can remember, and he really wants to share that love with his young audience. Pete lives in Saint Paul, Minnesota, with his wife, Leslie. They have two grown children and a small flock of lovely grandchildren.

Edited by Lily Coyle and Laurie Buss Herrmann

ISBN 13: 978-1-64343-847-4
Library of Congress Catalog Number: 2020909821
Printed in the United States of America
First Printing: 2020
24 23 22 21 20   5 4 3 2 1

Book design and typesetting by Sara J. Weingartner
Typefaces: nanum brush script, klee

Beaver's Pond Press
939 Seventh Street West
Saint Paul, MN 55102
(952) 829-8818
www.BeaversPondPress.com

To order, visit www.PeterRosscreates.com. Reseller discounts available.

Contact Peter Ross at www.PeterRosscreates.com for school visits, speaking engagements, freelance writing projects, and interviews.

To Ellen Green,
who showed me my book has wings to fly.

Uh-oh! Who didn't close the front door?
What kind of creatures have come to explore?
Oliver barely could find the right words.
Spiders, mice, ants? No! A house full of birds!

So many wild birds belonging outdoors.
They flew through the rooms and they waddled 'cross floors.

Wherever he looked, his house was infested.
He had to do something before the birds nested.

Oliver knew he could not work alone,
so he called Magic Mabel, who answered the phone.
"My magic method's the best anywhere.
In a jiffy I'll get those birds out of your hair!"

Oliver stared while awaiting assistance.
There were birds at his feet! There were birds in the distance!

Puffin in the kitchen was making a mess.
How she opened those sardines was anyone's guess.
Her colorful bill made her look like a clown.
Grinning with mischief, she slurped the meal down.

Ruffed grouse on pots and pans drummed loud and clear.
His wings beat like thunder. 'Twas heard far and near.

Grabbing two spoons Ollie started to pound.
Bada bing tink-tonk clang boom! Grouse don't dig that sound!

Oliver wanted these birds out the door,
though they were quite intriguing. Perhaps he'd learn more.
Northern saw-whet owl did not make a peep.
Her eyes were closed shut, for she wanted to sleep.

But the others were noisy. Owl might have to choose between joining the fun or taking a snooze.

Godwit and curlew were sharing a treat.
Oliver, curious, watched the pair eat.
Probing lime Jell-O with bills long and slender,
they picked all the fruit out, so juicy and tender.

A hummingbird pair, just as sweet as you please,
poked holes in the flour, then started to sneeze.
Flour's not part of a hummingbird's diet.
Those tiny birds' sneezes were remarkably quiet.

With a strong urge to run and no road to be found,
roadrunner hit on the best thing around.
Enjoying the treadmill, it ran for a while,
all in one place, mile after mile.

Said red-headed woodpecker, "Yellow is bland!"
Yellow-headed blackbird thought red should be banned.
A wise little nuthatch resolved the debate,
saying, "Beauty's within! All colors are great!"

Mallards and pelicans may not know math,
but they know only two birds should swim in one bath.
A snug little pond, the tub water was fine,
so mallard and pelican waited in line.

Kneeling at the side of the tub on a whim,
wearing his goggles to watch the ducks swim,
Oliver found the merganser quite flashy
and liked that the ruddy duck was very splashy!

Flocked round the television just down the hall,
cardinals and blue jays kept eyes on the ball.
Red birds and blue birds—their goal was the same.
No matter the outcome, they prized a good game.

A painting most dear to young Oliver's heart
was where two painted buntings got lost in the art.
Which prompted the buddies to try a new game.
They played hide-and-seek in the art in the frame.

Tanager, robin, and wren were all found,
with thrush and with bobolink hearing the sound
of an old record player that played a sweet song,
and soon all those songbirds were singing along.

Ollie sang too as he grinned a big grin,
sounding a bit like a smashed mandolin.
But he sang with great gusto, so joyful and proud.
(If you can't sing in tune, well, just sing really loud!)

Then a loud honking noise caught Ollie's ear.
What? Honking geese? No! Magic Mabel was here!

Her van held cool tools for all kinds of roles—
tall ladders, big nets, and extra-long poles.

Yet those tools for wrangling remained under locks.
All Mabel brought out was a brown cardboard box.
The box was plain, empty, and average in size.
"But it's magic," said Mabel, with twinkling eyes.

She set the box sideways down on the floor,
then tweeted bird calls from behind the big door.
With magical skills that were clearly superior,
her voice seemed to flow from the box's interior.

Her chirps, tweets, and whistles made such pleasant bait
that bird after bird came to investigate.
One by one they went in, looking for fun.
Somehow they all fit! Magic Mabel was done!

She picked up that box and took it outside,
and scattered its contents to range far and wide.

Birds on the water! Birds in the trees!
Birds near the flowers and birds in the breeze!

Birds in the green grass and birds on the sand.
Off went Magic Mabel with a wave of her hand.

Now all is well. Birds are where they belong.
Oliver's glad. What on earth could go wrong?

cast of **Feathered**

Ruffed Grouse

Ruby-throated Hummingbird

Atlantic Puffin

Long-billed Curlew

House Wren

Blue Jay

Northern Cardinal

Brown-headed Nuthatch

Hermit Thrush

Northern Saw-whet Owl

Bobolink

Greater Roadrunner